WHOPPERS

'Twould make an ox curl up
and die
To hear how Zek'l Pratt
would lie. . . .
Holman F. Day

WHOPPERS

Tall Tales and Other Lies

Collected from American Folklore
by ALVIN SCHWARTZ
Illustrated by GLEN ROUNDS

HarperCollins*Publishers*

Library of Congress Cataloging-in-Publication Data
Schwartz, Alvin, date comp.
  Whoppers.

  Bibliography: p.
  Summary: A collection of tall tales involving animals, the weather, narrow
escapes, and many other topics.
  1. Tales, American. [1. Folklore—United States] I. Rounds, Glen, date,
ill. II. Title.
PZ8.1.S399Wh   398.2'0973   74-32024
ISBN 0-397-31575-9. — ISBN 0-06-446091-6 (pbk.)

"I was tryin' t' git . . ." (pp. 39–41) is reprinted from *Ozark Mountain
Folks,* Vance Randolph, by permission of Vanguard Press, Inc. Copyright
1932 by Vanguard Press, Inc. Copyright renewed 1960 by Vance Randolph.
  "The events described . . ." (pp. 62–65) is reprinted from "Frozen
Death," Robert Wilson, an article in the *Old Farmer's Almanac,* 1943, and
in issues of *Yankee Magazine,* 1940, 1946, and 1963 by permission of Yankee,
Inc., Dublin, N.H. Copyright 1940, 1943, 1946, 1963 by Yankee, Inc.
  Every reasonable effort has been made to obtain appropriate permission
to reprint materials already in copyright. If the editor or publisher is notified
of omissions, corrections will be made in future editions.

For
Horse McSneed

CONTENTS

HARD LYING

To be truthful, this book is a pack of lies. I counted them just a minute ago and there are exactly one hundred and forty-five. I know thousands more, of course, but I didn't have room for them.

However, none are ordinary lies. Each is an outlandish tale about something that never happened and never could. And each is the work of a liar who lied for the fun of it.

In fact, often these liars used just enough of the truth to cause you to wonder if they *were* lying. But they exaggerated so, they seldom fooled anyone for long.

Folklorists call such tales lying tales or tall tales or, if they are very brief, just lies. But liars call them windies or whoppers or gallyfloppers. And when you tell one, they say you are spinning yarn or stretching a blanket or drawing a long bow.

If you really are good at lying, like my friend Horse McSneed, they will say you are a hard liar and that your lies are severe. This is the highest praise a liar can receive.

People have been telling such lies for as long as anyone knows. They do so because it is a pleasant way to pass the time. But years ago, those who lived on the frontier or in the backwoods also lied for another reason. When they told of beating a panther in a fist fight, or outracing a storm, or growing a pumpkin so big their cows used it as a barn, it made them feel stronger and made the hardships and the dangers easier to face. In fact, the bigger the problems they had, the bigger the lies they told.

If you plan to be a hard liar, there are a number of things you need to know. Be sure to tell each tale slowly, as if you were trying to make sure of every fact. And use enough facts so that, for a while, your lie will sound like the truth. And be deadly serious.

If anyone doubts what you say, tell him you were there, so you know it happened. Or tell him a close friend was there, and he would be glad to tell about it, except that he had to leave town.

Also bear in mind one other thing. Do not tell too many of these lying tales or you will suffer the fate of all hard liars. There will come a time when you do not know if you can believe yourself.

Alvin Schwartz

Princeton, New Jersey

WHOPPERS

1. ORDINARY PEOPLE

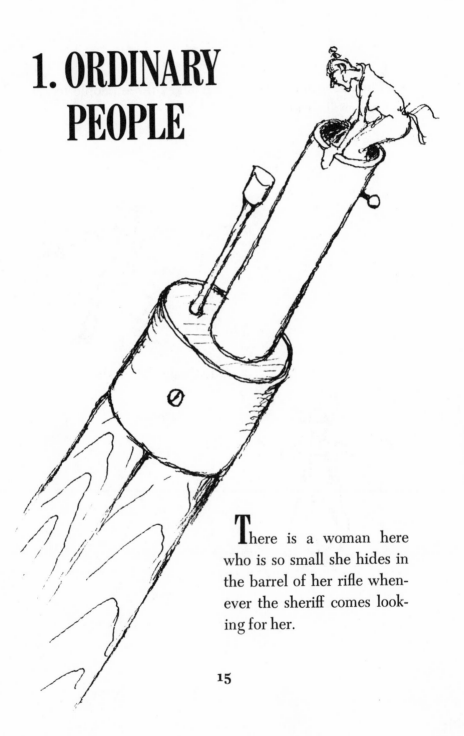

There is a woman here who is so small she hides in the barrel of her rifle whenever the sheriff comes looking for her.

Another woman is so fast it takes three people to see her when she runs:

One to say, "Here she comes!"

Another to say, "Here she is!"

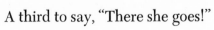

A third to say, "There she goes!"

And another is so tall she gets wet fifteen minutes before anybody else when it rains.

She is married to a man whose feet are so big he must put his pants on by pulling them over his head.

But he is so nimble he can stand a ladder
   straight
   up
   and
   down,
then climb to the top rung,
then pull the ladder up after him,
then climb it again.

And he is so strong he can pull himself three feet off the ground by his coat collar.

What gives him his strength is rock juice. He breaks boulders in half by spitting on them, then squeezes a glass of rock juice from the pieces, then drinks it.

His job is pulling crooked roads straight.

First he hooks a heavy chain to one end of a road, then he stretches the chain to the other end, then he yanks hard. When he finally gets the road the way he wants it, he sells the twists and turns to a town whose roads don't have any.

But he is a very stingy man. To save money he gives each of his children a penny if they do not eat their supper. Then he steals it back when they are asleep.

Yet he is so tenderhearted he cannot stand to see his wife work. As a result, whenever there is any work that must be done, he puts on his hat and goes to town.

2. ORDINARY THINGS

FARMING

Where the soil is *too* fertile, strange things happen.

There was this one farm, for example, where the farmer put in a cucumber patch, then headed for home. But he had taken no more than half a dozen steps when he heard what sounded like the boom of a cannon.

When he looked back, the air was filled with soil and stones, and cucumber vines were bursting from the ground and speeding in all directions like hungry snakes.

He began to run, but one vine soon caught up with him, then another did, and another. And before he knew it he was trapped in a twisting, writhing, ever-growing tangle.

Finally he managed to jerk one arm free and reached for his jackknife to cut himself loose. But a cucumber had sprouted in the pocket where he kept it and blocked his way. . . .

On a neighboring farm, a boy climbed a stalk of corn to fetch his mother six ears for dinner. But the stalk was growing so fast he found he could not get down.

When he called for help, his father came running and struck at the stalk with his ax, but it was growing with such speed he could not hit it twice in the same place.

Then two farmhands tried to cut it with a saw, but the

saw stuck in the stalk and disappeared into the gathering darkness.

By then the boy was out of sight, but the stalk kept growing.

To keep him from starving, each day his parents loaded a goose gun with biscuits and peas and shot them up to him.

Then they went home and prayed for a hard frost that would kill the stalk.

But cold weather was weeks away. . . .

There also are places where the soil is so miserable nobody can raise anything, not even a fuss.

On this one farm, the people are so poor all they eat is pancakes. And the pancakes are so thin they only have one side.

On another, they are so poor they feed their chickens sawdust instead of chicken feed. But that doesn't work too well. For some of the chickens lay eggs with splinters. And others lay knotholes.

FIDDLING

There is this fiddle that is so big it takes two horses to draw the bow across the strings. And when they stop, the fiddle goes on humming for six weeks more. It's worth seeing. And it's just a few miles from here, or it was the other day.

FIGHTING

There were these two old-timers who had some trouble with each other, but they couldn't get it settled no matter what.

Since they both were crack shots with their rifles, about the best in the whole country, they figured the only way to take care of it quick and no fooling was with a duel.

So they went off into the woods all by themselves and turned back to back, and each of them stepped off twenty paces and turned around.

Then they counted up to three and fired. But blame if either one of them even got creased.

At first they felt sort of ashamed at missing such an easy shot and just stood there brooding. But after a while they got to remembering the trouble they'd had and how much they hated each other, so they tried again. But they didn't have any luck that time either.

Well, they were so determined to kill each other they

just kept trying. But no matter how much care they took, each time they fired they missed. And at last they just gave up.

Naturally, it kind of bothered them to call it off that way, but there wasn't much they could do about it.

Anyway, as they walked toward each other to shake hands, one of them stepped on something red-hot, and

he let out a holler. And when they looked down they saw a big lump of sizzling lead.

Those two old buzzards had shot so straight and true that each pair of bullets they fired met midway between, then melted from the heat and dropped to the ground. It's a fact.

These two other men also had an argument. One was named Bob. The other called himself the Child of Calamity.

Right off, Bob jumped into the air, cracked his heels together once, and shouted:

"Whoo-oop!

"I'm the old original iron-jawed, brass-mounted, copper-bellied corpse-maker. Look at me! I'm the man they call Sudden Death!

"Look at me! I take nineteen alligators for breakfast when I'm in robust health, and a bushel of rattlesnakes and a dead body when I'm ailing! I split the everlasting rocks with my glance, and I squench the thunder when I speak!

"Whoo-oop!

"Stand back and give me room! Blood's my natural drink and the wails of the dying is music to my ears! Lay low, for I'm 'bout to turn myself loose!"

Then the Child of Calamity jumped into the air, cracked his heels *three times*, and told for five minutes what a powerful, dangerous, bloodthirsty, miserable wretch *he* was.

Then they punched each other, mostly in the face. Then Bob called the Child names, and the Child called Bob names back again. Next, Bob called him a heap rougher names, and the Child come back at him with the very worst kind of language.

Next Bob knocked the Child's hat off, and the Child picked it up and knocked Bob's hat off and kicked it about six feet.

Bob went and got it and said never mind, this warn't going to be the last of this, because he was a man that never forgot and never forgive, and so the Child better look out, for he would have to answer to him with the best blood in his body.

The Child said he was giving Bob fair warning never to cross his path again, for he could never rest until he had waded in Bob's blood—though he was sparing him now on account of his family, if he had one.

The Spang-Fired Truth About Chester Cahoon

The thund'rinest fireman the Lord ever made
Was Chester Cahoon of the Tuttsville Brigade. . . .
To see him you'd think he was daft as a loon,
But that was jest habit with Chester Cahoon. . . .

There was the time of the fire at Jenkins' old place.
It got a big start—was a desprit case;
The fambly they didn't know which way to turn.
And by gracious, it looked like it all was to burn.
But Chester Cahoon—oh, that Chester Cahoon,
He sailed to the roof like a reg'lar balloon . . .
And five minutes later that critter he came
To the second floor winder surrounded by flame.
He lugged in his arms . . . a stove and a bed,
And balanced a bureau right square on his head.
His hands they was loaded with crockery stuff,
China and glass; as if that warn't enough,
He'd rolls of big quilts 'round his neck like a wreath,
And carried Mis' Jenkins' old aunt with his teeth.
You're right—just as right as can be. . . . Didn't seem
The critter'd get down, but he called for the stream *

* The hose.

HERO

And when it come strong and . . . round as my wrist
He stuck out his legs and give 'em a twist;
And he hooked round the water as if 'twas a rope
And down he come easin' himself on the slope. . . .

A fishing guide named Ed Grant told this tale to Francis I. Maule in 1904 or thereabouts at a fishing camp in Maine.

"Nine years ago the eleventh of last June, I was fishin' out there in the lily pads, and right under the third yaller leaf to the right of the channel—yes, that one with the rip in it—I ketched a trout 'bout six inches long.

"Never did see a more intelligent-lookin' little feller— high forehead, smooth face, round, dimpled chin, and a most uncommon bright, sparklin', knowin' eye.

"I always allowed that with patience and cunning a real young trout (when they get to ten or fifteen pounds there ain't no teachin' them nothin') could be tamed like a dog or cat.

"When I go ashore I gets a tub to keep him in. But first I bores a little hole through the side close to the bottom and stops the hole with a peg. Then I fills the tub with water.

"Every night after the little feller gets asleep, I pulls out the peg and lets out jest a little of the water. I does this night after night so mighty sly he never suspects nothin'.

"After he lived hale and hearty and dry on the bottom of the tub for three weeks, I knowed he was fit for trainin'.

"So I took him out and let him wiggle for a while on

34

the path and soon got to feedin' him out of my hand. Pretty soon after that, he could foller me right good all around the clearin'.

"Well, as time went on, he got to follerin' me most everywhere and hardly ever lost sight of me, and me and him were great friends.

"Near about sundown one evening, I went out to the brook back of the camp to get some butter out of a pail, and, of course, he comes trottin' along behind.

"Well, sir, he follered me close up and came out onto the logs we used to cross the brook, and jest as I was a-stoopin' down over the pail I heard a 'kee-plunk!' And Gorry! if he hadn't slipped through a chink between them logs and was drownded before I could reach him."

There was this man who caught such a big fish that the picture he took of it weighed twelve pounds.

In those days I was billed as Billie the Dolphin, the spectacular, death-defying high diver. I was working with Miller's Great Exposition Shows, using a twenty-five-foot ladder and diving into a tank of water ten feet deep.

Big crowds came to see me. And not a soul ever seemed dissatisfied until one night when I happened to

36

be playing in the same town as Eddie La Breen, the Human Seal, who worked for Barker's Shows.

As I climbed out of the tank that night I heard somebody say, "That ain't nothin'. You ought to go see Eddie La Breen. He dives from fifty feet into five feet of water."

Well, it was true. And I was told to dive fifty feet or else. It sure looked high when I got up there, and I could feel my nose scraping the bottom after I dove in. But Eddie La Breen wasn't going to outdo me if I could help it.

Then Eddie sends word that I might as well stop trying. "I'm going to dive from a thousand feet while playing the ukelele and eating raw liver," he said.

Well, he didn't exactly do that, but he did raise his ladder to one hundred feet, then dove into two feet of water.

Well, I practiced and practiced—I really needed that job—and I made it from one hundred and fifty feet into one foot of water.

Then Eddie sent word he was going to change his name from the Human Seal to the Minnow.

"You know how a minnow just skitters along the top of a pond," he said. "Well, that's the way I'll land in that water. From two hundred feet, I'm going to dive into six inches, then skitter off without making a bubble." And he did it.

Well, I did that minnow dive too, except that I dived into four inches from two hundred and fifty feet and didn't even muss my hair.

Then Eddie made dives from three hundred feet into *three* inches. Of course, when that happened, I was a little put out. But I told them to get me a good thick bath mat and soak it all day in water and I'd dive into that from three hundred and fifty feet.

Well, the first time I hit the mat it sort of knocked me dizzy. But I got better and better at it until it didn't bother me hardly at all.

But after I reached three fifty, Eddie wouldn't go any higher. It was just too much for him and, sad to say, he lost his job.

Yet I beat him fair and square. He just wasn't man enough to admit it. And not only was he jealous, he was treacherous. But I didn't learn that until quite a while later.

They had soaked the mat as usual that day. But they must have let it out of their sight because somebody squeezed all the water out of it and wrung it dry. And when I dived into it that night it was like diving into a block of concrete.

Later somebody said that a man who looked like Eddie La Breen had been lurking around the show grounds. Now, if he didn't do it, who did?

HUNTING

The way Ab Yancey tells it, this is what happened that day.

"I was tryin' t' git two red squirrels lined up so's I could kill both of 'em with one bullet. I reckon I must o' sot thar twenty minutes a-waitin'. But when I pulled the trigger I got 'em.

"Jest then I heerd wild turkeys a-yoikin' an' I looked an' seen seven hens an' a gobbler a-settin' in a tree, not movin'. Seems like that bullet skittered over thar some way an' split th' limb they was a-settin' on, an' ketched their feet in th' crack!

"Wal, sir, I clumb up t' git them turkeys afore they bust loose, but jest as I was a-comin' down I lost my holt an' fell slap-dab in a bresh pile. Thar I was a-scramblin' an' a-rollin', an' afore I could git out I'd smothered a hull gang o' quails an' two big swamp-rabbits!

"Then I tied them eight turkeys an' them forty-one quails an' them two swamp-rabbits all t'gether an' back I went to whar my squirrels was at.

"One o' them had fell in th' creek, so I waded in atter him. But hit was deeper 'n I figgered. An' when I got out, danged if my pockets and boot tops wasn't jest chuck full o'fish—mostly pearch an' goggle-eye.

"Whilst I was a-stringin' them, I retch back 't scratch a chigger bite, an' one o' th' buttons on my shirt popped off'n hit. I seen th' danged thing go a-whistlin' off into a bunch o' hazel bresh, an' I aimed for t' hunt it up soon as I got my fish strung.

"But d'rectly I heerd a turrible scufflin' an' gaspin' an' gurglin', so I drapped th' fish an' snuck over whar I could peek in. Thar was a big buck deer a-rollin' round, an' he was a-dyin', but danged if I could see what kilt him. Hit kinda skeered me.

"But I jest cut his throat anyhow, t' let him bleed right good, an' thar was my ol' button stuck in his windpipe! He must of opened up his mouth for t' belch an' that button jest flipped in thar an' shut his wind plumb off.

"Hit shore was th' biggest one-bullet huntin' I ever done, seen, or hearn tell of. Thar was one deer, eight turkeys, two squirrels, two swamp-rabbits, forty-one quail, an' maybe fifty pound o' fish, an' Pappy shore was proud when he seen me a-draggin' all of hit home.

"Hit was a sad day at our place, though, on account of Uncle Hen. Uncle Hen was a purty good feller, but he didn't have no sense. An' he up an' called me a liar when I was a-tellin' how I got that 'ar buck.

"'Liar' allus was a fightin' word in th' Yancey family, so I jest naturally had t' kill him. Pap hisse'f said he couldn't blame me none.

"I done it with my ol' huntin' knife—same one you see a-stickin' out o' my boot top right now."

This artist was so talented that when he painted a dog it bit him.

But he should have known better. Earlier he had painted a snowstorm and caught cold.

PROSPECTING FOR SILVER

Well," said this prospector, "the richest strike I ever made was one time when I was by myself. I saw a bluff 'bout three miles off that had a queer look to it.

"When I got over there I found it was a thousand feet high and almost solid silver. You could follow it for a mile and see nothin' else."

"Then how come you're so poor?"

"Well, I got back to camp in a day's ride an' was packin' up one mornin' after breakfast. When I came to my fryin' pan, my mule had one foot in it, an' I tapped him on the leg to make him step outen it, an' he up an' kicked me in the head."

"But he didn't break your head, did he?"

"No, but I can't remember directions since."

PULLING TEETH

This old doctor in Demijohnville has seen hard times in his day, especially in pulling teeth.

One case he says he will never forget involved a fellow named Barney who had a bad toothache and sent for him one Sunday morning.

Usually this doctor used a hammer and a nail to pry a tooth loose. But when that didn't work, he cut away the gum around Barney's tooth and fastened a piece of stout twine to it. Next he tied Barney's feet to a large ring bolted to the barn floor.

Then the doctor took hold of the twine. And Barney's wife took hold of the doctor's coattail. And the rest of the family lined up one behind the other. Then they all pulled as hard as they could, but they could not move the tooth.

Later some people who were passing by joined in, but the tooth still would not budge.

At noon a lot of people on their way home from church also hitched on, until the line extended over the hill and into the swamp.

When they all pulled together, Barney was whipped off his feet and stretched flat in the air as if he were flying.

Suddenly he cried, "Stop!" and the whole line fell over backward. Everybody thought the tooth finally had come out, but instead his head had come off.

When the doctor examined the tooth, he found that its roots went down the whole length of Barney's body and were fastened in the bottom of one of his feet. He says it was the hardest case he ever had.

3. FANCY CLOTHES AND NARROW ESCAPES

WHERE JOE MERRIWEATHER WENT TO

Joe Merriweather was a dressy sort of feller. He owned a coat with brass buttons, a bright red neckerchief, a pair of buckskin britches with straps that fitted under his boots, and other sporty stuff.

That particular day Joe was wearing those buckskin britches. He and his brother Bill had been drenched by a heavy rain and had made a big fire on the riverbank to dry themselves. Usually buckskin stretches when it gets wet, then shrinks as it dries. But as Joe's britches began to dry and shrink, a strange thing happened.

"All ov a sudden," Bill recalled, "I thought the little feller was a-growin' uncommon tall. Then I diskivered those buckskin britches wur beginnin' to shrink and

those straps under his boots wur beginnin' to lift Brother
Joe off the ground.

"'Brother Joe,' sez I, 'you're a-goin' up.'

"'Brother Bill,' sez he, 'I ain't a-doin' anythin' else.'

"Then he scrunched down mighty hard; but it warn't
ov no use, fur afor long he wur a matter of some fifteen
feet up in the air.

"'Brother Joe,' sez I.

"'I'm here,' sez he.

"'Catch hold ov the top ov that tree,' sez I.

"He sorter leaned over and grabbed the saplin'. But it warn't ov no use, fur it gradually begun to give way at the roots, and afor he'd got five foot higher, it jist slipped out er the ground.

" 'Brother Joe,' sez I.

" 'I'm a list'nin',' sez he.

" 'Cut your straps!' sez I, for I seed it was his last chance.

"He outs with his jackknife, and leanin' over sideways makes a rip at the sole of his left foot. There was a considerable deal ov cracklin' fur a second or two, then a crash sorter like as if a waggon-load ov wood had bruck down, and the fust thing I know'd t'other leg shot up and started him movin'.

"And the last thing I seed ov Brother Joe, he was a-whirlin' round like a four-spoked wheel with the rim off, away over toward sundown!"

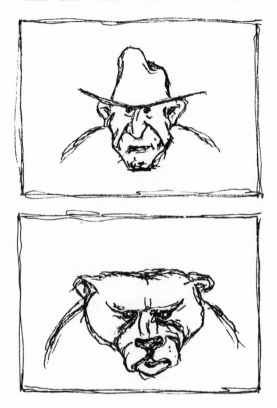

This old man was a peaceable sort, but for some reason bears seemed to pick on him.

"I was walking in the woods one day," he recalled, "when a big black bear charged at me with its mouth wide open.

"Since I had nothing to defend myself with, I jammed my arm down the bear's throat all the way to where the

49

stump of its tail joined its body. Then I grabbed hold of the stump and yanked as hard as I could and pulled that bear inside out. Of course, this turned it in the other direction and frightened it so it ran off.

"Another time, it was in July, I was picking raspberries when I looked up and saw—at the far end of the field—another bear.

"This time I didn't have any weapons either. But since I had a good start, I decided to run for it. And since the bear was hungry, it came tearing right along after me.

"We ran through field after field and through forest after forest, up hill and down dale, mile after mile, on and on and on. Finally we came to a river which I quickly crossed on the ice. But the bear was too heavy and it fell through and drowned."

"How come there was ice on the river in July?" somebody asked.

"Oh," he said, "I forgot to tell you. We had done so much running, by then it was December."

No sooner had I marked off a little spot for a home than the Injins 'vaded my peaceful homicil and kidnumped me. After wavin' thar tommyhocks over my knowledge-box, and then thar butcher knives, they helt a council and decided my time had come.

So they got a bar'l, tuck out the top, stuck me in, and closed it tight, all 'ceptin' the bunghole fur me to get ar.* Then they left me to starve.

I soon got a-hongory—I allers had a rantankerous appertite—and thought of uvrything to eat, good and bad, in all creation. But it only whetted my gizzard to think of it.

So I determined to git out'n thar and pounded away with my fist till I beat it nairly to jelly. Then I butted a spell with my noggin. But it were no go.

So I caved in, made my last will and testerment, and

* A bunghole is a small opening near the bottom of a barrel, through which small amounts of oil or molasses or some other liquid can be drawn.

vartually gin up the ghost. It were a mighty serious time with me, fur sure.

While I were lyin' thar, I hearn suthin' scrambulatin' in the leaves and snortin' like he didn't adzackly care for what he smelt. I lay still as a salamander and thought, "Maybe there is a chance for Stanley yit."

So the critter, whatever it mout be, kept moseyin' round the bar'l. Last he come to the bunghole, put his nose in, and giv a monstrous loud snort. I soon seen it were a bar.

Thinks I, "Old feller, look out! Old Oliver ain't dade yit!" Jist then he put his big black paw in as fur as he could and scrabbled 'bout to make some 'scovery.

The fust thing that struck my noggin was to nab his paw, but I soon seen that wouldn't do. So I jist waited a spell, with great flutterbation of mind.

His next move was to put his tail in the bunghole to test its innards. And that were my chance. So I seized holt and shouted at the top of my voice:

"On, Stanley, on!"

And on we went, bar'l and all, the bar at full speed. Now my hope were that he would jump over some presserpuss, brake the bar'l all to shiverations, and liberate me from my nasty, stinkin' prison.

And sure nuff, he leaped over a waterfall fifty foot high. And down he went in a pile bustin' the bar'l all to flinderations, nairly shockin' my gizzard out'n me.

I've nuther seen nur hearn from that bar since, but he has my best wishes for his present and future welfar.

THE TRAP

This cowboy was out riding one day and suddenly plunged into a deep hole, with walls as straight and smooth as glass, and no way out but up.

His horse was badly injured and quickly died. Although the cowboy was not hurt, he soon ran out of food and water, and as the days passed he grew weaker and more desperate.

With the smell of death in the air, hordes of buzzards arrived. At first they made wide sweeps over the hole. Then they circled lower and lower until, finally, one landed right next to the cowboy. However, the buzzard ignored him. For it was the horse that it wanted now.

But that bird gave the cowboy an idea. Working as fast as he could, he unraveled his lariat and cut the thin strands of twine into pieces about twelve feet long. At the end of each he tied a small loop.

He then sneaked up behind the buzzard, slipped a loop around one of its legs, and tied the other end of the line to his belt.

Each time another buzzard landed he did the same thing. After he had harnessed about twenty this way, he fired his last bullet into the air. This so startled the buzzards they took off—and took him with them.

When they had hauled him free of his trap, he unbuckled his belt and dropped to the ground. But as luck would have it, he landed up to his neck in mud and had to walk a mile to get a shovel to dig himself out.

HALFWAY

Have you heard about the man who swam halfway across the ocean, then decided he couldn't make it and swam back?

BOOTS

Rattlesnakes? Yes, sir; I *have* seen rattlesnakes. Some years ago I grew tired of sailing the seas and took a farm. I had a meadow on the prairie of three hundred acres. And when it came to haying time, the rattlesnakes were so thick, five of the seven men I sent to mow were bitten and died instantly."

"And you lost your hay?"

"Not at all. I have seen too much of snakes to be bluffed off by them. I owned a pair of boots of the kind worn by the Gauchos when they go to hunt the jaguar. They were made of the toughest bull's hide, doubled, and they came up to my hips. I was confident that if they could resist the jaguar's claws, they could resist the fangs of the rattlesnake.

"I put them on one fine morning and with a scythe went to the meadow and began to mow. The snakes came at me a dozen at a time, but whenever they struck their fangs into the leather it held them fast.

56

"I took no notice of them, but kept mowing until they hung in such numbers from my legs that the weight became troublesome. Then I stopped mowing and cut them off with the scythe. I had to do this about every half hour. When I went home to dinner there were so many heads hanging from the boots, you hardly could see the leather.

"I kept this up for a fortnight. By that time, I can tell you, snakes were getting scarce in our meadow."

"What became of the boots?"

"Them boots saved my life not long afterward. You see, I soon got tired of farming and went to sea again. I bought a brig and started on a trading expedition to the west coast of Africa.

"Off the Cape de Verdes we had the worst storm I ever saw in my life and went aground on a reef a little south of Cape Blanco, where the Great Desert comes down to the sea.

"The next day a whole tribe of Arabs appeared on the beach making signals to us. I went ashore to see what they wanted, as I did not like to expose the boat's crew to harm. But first I put on them boots in order that I might wade from the boat to the beach.

"As soon as I landed I was seized and hurried over some sand hills to their camp. Knowing enough of their language to understand what they were saying, I found that they meant to trick my crew into coming ashore, make slaves of them, and plunder the ship.

"As part of this plan they treated me decently for a time, only taking my boots. This seemed odd at first.

But I soon found that they were almost wholly out of food, although they had plenty of water, and that they meant to make soup of the boots.

"They put them in a big pot over the fire, and in about an hour invited me to share the broth. I declined, and they ate it themselves.

"In half an hour every mother's son of them was as dead as Julius Caesar. There was enough rattlesnake poison in those boots, sir, to destroy everyone everywhere.

"The next day we got the brig off the reef without serious damage and found enough gold dust in that camp to make every member of the crew a rich man. That was on the whole the most successful voyage I ever made."

UNCLE DAVY LANE
LOSES HIS UNDERWEAR

While I was moseyin' about, I cum right chug upon one uv the biggest, longest, outdaciousest snakes I uver laid my peepers on. He rared right straight up, like a Maypole, licked out his tarnacious tongue, and good as said, 'Here's at you, sir. What bizness have you on my grit?'

"Now I'd hearn folks say ef you'd look a poisonous animal right plump in the eyes he couldn't hurt you. Now, I tried it good. But bless you, honey! He had no more respect for me than he had fur a huckleberry. So I seed that I'd have to move on quick.

"I jumped 'bout ten steps the first leap and turned my noggin round to look for the critter. Thar he were right dab at my heels, head up, tongue out, and his eyes like two balls uv fire. I 'creased my verlocity, clarin' thick bushes, bushheaps, deep gullies, and branches.

"Again I looked back, thinkin' I had sartinly left the sarpunt a long gap behind. And what do you think? Thar he were! So I moved on faster 'n uver.

" 'Twasn't long afore I run out'n my shirt, then out'n my britches, then out'n my drawers. Thinks I, surely the sarpunt are distanced now.

"But thar he were! I jumped about thirty-five foot, screamed like a wildcat, and 'creased my verlocity at a

monstrous rate. Jist then I begun to feel my skin split, and, thinks I, it's no use to run out'n my skin as humin skin are scarce.

"But by this time I'd run clean beyont my house, right smack through my yard, scaring Molly, the childering, the dogs, cats, chickens—uvry thing—half to death.

"But I got rid of my inimy, fur the sarpunt had respect for my house even if he didn't have respect fur me."

The events described were found recorded in a local diary. They were verified by an old man who said his father was among those who had been operated on. As far as is known, the practice is no longer followed today.

January 7—I went on the mountains and witnessed what to me was a horrible sight. It seems that people here who are old or handicapped, and are unable to help support their families, are "put away" for the winter months.

I will describe what I saw. Six persons—four men and two women—had been put to sleep with medicines and lay on the dirt floor of a cabin while members of their families gathered about them.

In a short time the unconscious bodies were inspected by a man who said: "They are ready."

They were stripped of their clothing except for a single garment. Then they were carried outside, placed on logs, and exposed to the freezing mountain air.

Soon their fingers, noses, and ears began to turn white; then their faces, arms, and legs did. I could stand the cold no longer and went inside where I found their families in cheerful conversation.

After an hour or so I went out again and looked at the bodies once more. By then they were freezing fast.

When I returned to the cabin, the men were smoking their pipes. But instead of talking cheerfully, as they had before, they were silent. Perhaps they were thinking that the time would come when they would be carried out the same way.

I passed the dreary night terror-stricken by the sights I had witnessed.

January 8—By now the six bodies were completely frozen.

After breakfast, a number of men went into the forest to cut hemlock and spruce boughs. Meanwhile, others nailed together a rough box about ten feet long and about five feet high and five feet wide.

When they finished they lined the box with two feet of straw, carefully placed three of the bodies inside, and covered them with a cloth and more straw. Then they placed the other bodies on top of the first and covered them the same way. Finally, they nailed the tomb shut.

By this time the other men had returned with the spruce and hemlock boughs with which they covered the box. Within weeks, twenty feet of snow or more would cover the boughs and the box.

"We shall want our people to help us plant corn next spring," the wife of one of the frozen men told me. "If you want to see them awaken, come back about the tenth day of next May."

May 10—I arrived here at ten o'clock in the morning after riding for four hours over rough, muddy roads. The weather is warm and pleasant. Most of the snow is gone, except where there are drifts.

The people I left last January were now ready to remove the bodies. The men began working at once, shoveling the snow from around the box, then hauling away the brush. When the box was clear, they pried off the cover.

Then they removed the frozen, lifeless bodies and placed each in a trough of warm water, with their heads raised slightly. To each trough they added large quantities of boiling water.

After soaking for about an hour, the bodies lost their white color and began to look more normal. At that point everyone began to vigorously massage them. This continued for over an hour, until the "frozen dead" began to gasp for breath and their muscles began to twitch.

Their families then trickled small quantities of drink down their throats, increasing the amount as they seemed better able to swallow.

After a while they opened their eyes and began to talk haltingly. Then, with the help of their loved ones, they sat up.

Finally they were helped to the cabin, dressed in

warm clothes, and fed a hearty meal. They seemed in no way injured. In fact, they appeared well refreshed by their long winter's sleep.

CHUNKEY'S FIGHT WITH THE PANTERS

I'd taken a wrong arm of the lake and war lost. It had commenced gettin' dark; the wind were blowin' and groanin'; the black clouds were flyin'; an' I were goin' along sorter oneasy when a panter yelled out close to me.

"I turned with my gun cocked, but I didn't see nothin'. Presently I hearn the panter again. Then I seen it and also one of its friends.

" 'Is that you?' said I, takin' a quick shot, and missin', but scarin' them off for a bit.

"I quickly drapp'd my gun to reload, but when I looked in my gourd there barely were enough powder for one shot more. So I loaded up mighty careful with what little I had.

"Then I started lookin' fer a holler tree to sleep in. But every now and then I'd git a glimpse of those panters follerin' me, makin' arrangements to have my scalp tonight.

" 'Panters,' says I, 'I'll make a bargain. If you let *me* alone, I will let *you* alone—and if you don't, I've got a gun fer one of you and this knife here fer the other!

"But now my knife was missin'!

"Well, I thought I war witched! Well, I did! Oh, you may larph. But just imagine yourself on Sky Lake in cane thirty feet high, three miles wide, thirty miles long,

66

thick as the har on a dog's back, and out o' powder, and your knife gone, and you hungry and tired, and two panters follerin' you. And you'd think you was witched, too.

"Two or three times I thought they'd gone, but presently they'd be back. Then I'd shout at 'em and away they'd go fer a bit.

"I knowed it wouldn't do to risk a fight in all that cane. So I pushed on to find an open place whar I could use my last shot, then—if I had to—try to smash 'em with my gun.

"Presently I found a place whar I determined to fight it out.

"And soon here they come again. If a stranger had seen 'em, he'd a' thought they were playin'. They'd jump and squat and bend their backs, and lay down and roll, and grin like puppies.

"But each time they came back they got closer and closer, and each time it was gettin' darker and darker. And I knowed I had to use my gun mighty soon or I couldn't see to shoot.

"So I raised up and fired. One of 'em sprung into the air and give a yell. The other came at me like a streak. Then she stopped and began slowly creepin' toward me —her ears laid back, her eyes turnin' green and sorter swimmin' around like, and the end of her tail twistin' like a snake.

"Then I seen her slippin' her legs underneath and knew she was goin' to spring. So I pulled back my gun to smash her when she come, but I missed—and she had me!

"Rip, rip, rip—and 'way went my blanket, my coat, and my britches. Then she sunk her teeth deep into my shoulder, her green eyes close to mine, the froth from her mouth flyin' in my face, and warm blood runnin' down my side.

"*Moses!* How fast she did fight!

"Then I seen she were arter my throat—and with that I grabbed *hern,* and commenced slamming my fist into her side, like cats a-fightin'.

"Rip, rip—she'd take me! Diff, slam, bang—I'd gin it to her! She fightin' for her supper, I fightin' for my life!

"Well, we had it round and round, sometimes one on top, then yother, she a-growlin' and I a-gruntin'! We had both commenced gettin' mighty tired, and presently she made a spring—but in the opposite direction from me, *tryin' to git away!*

" 'Oh, ho!' says I, hittin' her a lick every time I spoke. 'You are willin' to quit even and divide stakes, are you?' Then round and round we went again.

"But presently she broke my hold. And I fell one way and she yother.

"Then she darted into the cane. And that's the last time I ever hearn of *that* panter!

"When I sorter came to myself, I war struttin' and thunderin' like a big he-gobbler, and then I commenced examinin' to see what harm she'd done me. I war bit powerful in the shoulder and arm—jist look at them scars!—but when I found thar were no danger of its killin' me, I set to braggin'.

" 'Oh, you ain't dead yet, Chunkey,' says I. 'You have whipped a panter in a fair fight.' Then I cock-a-doodle-dood a spell for joy!"

JIM GOT MURDERED

Hallo, Jim. Is that you?"
"This is what's left of me."
"Well, I'd heard you'd been murdered."
"So did I. But I knew it was a lie as soon as I heard it."

4. ANIMALS AND INSECTS

CATS

There was a trapper used to live out back here in the woods, and every winter he set a lot of traps. He had a cat that used to follow him around, and that cat got to be such a good hunter he got all his food out in the woods. The trapper didn't have to feed him at all. In fact, the cat got so he wouldn't eat anythin' unless he had killed it himself.

One day when the cat was out huntin', he got one of his front paws caught in a trap. When the trapper finally found him, that paw was so bad he had to cut most of it off. It healed all right, but the cat kept getting thinner and thinner because he wouldn't eat the food the trapper gave him.

The trapper decided he'd have to do somethin' or he'd lose that cat for sure. So he whittled out a small wooden leg and tacked some leather on it to fit over the stump of

the cat's thigh. Then he cut some leather straps to go around the cat's body and hold the leg in place.

At first the cat kept shakin' his paw to try to get the thing off. But by and by he got used to it and got so he could prance around in great style. Soon after, he started to fatten up, so the trapper knew he was huntin' again.

But what he didn't know was how on earth that cat managed to do it. So one day he followed him. What that animal did was creep up on somethin', then grab it with one paw, then hit it over the head with that wooden leg.

DOGS

There was this competition to see who had the fastest, toughest hunting dog around. When Larkin Snow entered Flyin'-jib, everybody hooted and laughed, for he was just a runt of an animal. But Larkin knew what his dog could do and didn't say anything.

Right after they started out, the dogs scared up a fox that took off like greased lightning. For a while most of them kept up with him pretty well. But soon Flyin'-jib and that fox were charging through a field a half mile ahead of the pack and pulling away. It was then that it happened.

As Larkin tells it, "Thar were a mowin'-scythe in that meadder with the blade standin' up. And Flyin'-jib run chug aginst it with sich force that it split him wide open frum the end uv his nose to the tip uv his tail. Thar he lay, and nuver whimpered, jist tryin' to run straight on.

"I streaked to him, snatched up both sides, and slapped 'um together. But I were in sich a hurry I put two feet down and two feet up. But away he went anyhow.

"You see, when he got tired runnin' on two feet, he'd jist whirl over, quick as lightnin', and run on t'other two. It seemed to increase his verlocity. Fer he cotch the fox a mile ahead uv the whole kit uv 'um.

"Now when the fellers come up and seen all thar dogs lyin' on the ground pantin' fur life and Flyin'-jib fresh as a daisy, they was mighty low down in the mouth. But I just kervorted and told 'um that were the way fur a dog to run fast and long, fust one side up, then t'other—it rested him."

After Larkin stuck Flyin'-jib together that way, people said the dog barked out of both ends of his body. But Larkin never claimed *that*.

The hogs on this farm are so thin and scrawny they have to stand in the same place twice to cast a shadow.

And they are so weak it takes a half dozen of them to pull up a blade of grass. One seizes the blade in his mouth, then the rest take one another by the tail, and they all pull together.

MOSQUITOES

In some places the mosquitoes are so big that one can whip a dog, two can overcome a man, and four can fly off with a cow.

One time a swarm of mosquitoes with stingers two feet long attacked a farmer in a field. As protection, he grabbed for a large iron pot that happened to be nearby and pulled it over himself. But the mosquitoes drilled holes through the metal.

As their stingers came through, he bent them back with a hammer he had. But with a mighty tug they raised the pot from the ground and flew off with it.

A few days later another farmer found it and hung it from a branch, and filled it with water, and used it as a shower bath.

Another time a man asleep in his bed was awakened by what sounded like people talking. But in a corner of his room were two large figures he recognized as mosquitoes.

"He looks mighty tasty," said one. "Should we eat him here or should we take him home?"

"Let's eat him here," said the other. "If we take him home, the big guys will grab him and eat him."

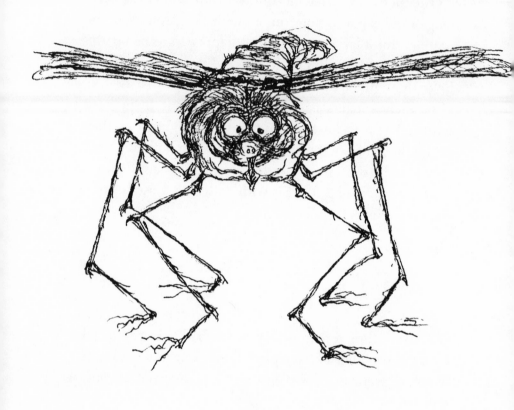

Still another time, the largest mosquito anyone had ever seen threatened to destroy this village.

Because of a long drought there were few animals left in the marsh where he lived, and the blood he needed for food was almost gone.

Close to starvation, he headed for the village, eating almost every living thing in his path—horses, cows, goats, pigs, chickens, people.

As he approached, the villagers began to flee. Meanwhile, the leading citizens debated over what to do.

The local doctor proposed that they feed a worthless cow all the poison she would eat, then tie her in the road as bait for the oncoming monster. If he ate her, he would die, the doctor said.

The cow was fed the poison and tied in place. A short while later the mosquito arrived and ate her. But he was so strong that the poison did not have the slightest effect on him.

In fact, when he had finished with the cow, he saw a tough old mule grazing nearby. And he ate him, too.

But the mule kicked so hard on the way down that he broke the mosquito's neck, and the village was saved. And so was the mule.

SNAKES

These two snakes had a fight. After circling for a while, one grabbed the other's tail and started swallowing it. Then the other grabbed the first snake's tail and started swallowing *it*. By the time they finished, they had swallowed each other.

A man walking along a country road saw a big rattlesnake pinned under a rock. He immediately lifted the rock and freed the snake.

The snake was so grateful it followed him home. When the man's family tried to drive it away, it refused to go. Eventually they gave up and accepted it as a family pet and allowed it to sleep in the family bedroom.

All this time the snake tried to find some way to repay the man's kindness. Finally one night its chance came.

When everyone was asleep, a burglar crept in through the window. Sensing danger to those he loved, the snake darted across the floor and coiled itself tightly around him. Then it stuck its tail out the window and rattled for the police, who came on the run.

SPIDERS

The Santa Fe is the most dangerous spider in the whole world.

It has one hundred legs with a stinger on each, and a forked tail with two large stingers, and fangs bigger than a rattlesnake's.

If it stings you with its legs, you might last an hour. If it stings you with all its stingers, you might last fifteen minutes.

But if it stings you and bites you at the same time, you have only five minutes to live. First you will turn blue, then yellow, then a beautiful bright green. Then your hair will fall out. Then you will drop dead as a doornail.

5. PUTREFACTIONS AND OTHER WONDERS

A PUTRIFIED FOREST

I was out on the Black Hills—it was the year it rained fire, and everybody knows when that was. The snow was about fifty foot deep and the buffler lay dead on the ground. Not whar we were tho', for *thar* we had no buffler, and no meat, and fer six weeks me and my band had been livin' on our moccasins.*

"But one day we crossed a canyon and a divide and thar were green grass, and green trees, and birds singing in the green leaves, and *this* in February.

"When they seen the green grass, our animals was like to die for joy, and we all sung out, 'Hurraw for summer doin's!'

" 'Hyar goes fer meat,' says I, and I jest ups my rifle at one of them singing birds and down comes the critter, its head spinning away from its body. But it never stops singing, and when I pick it up I find it is stone.

---

* Which meant chewing on the soles of the moccasins, which were made of buffalo hide, for any nourishment they had left in them.

"Then Rube takes his ax and lets drive at a cottonwood tree. Schr-u-k— goes the ax agin' the tree, and out comes a bit of the blade as big as my hand.

"We looks at the animals and thar they stood just staring at the grass, which I'm dog-gone if it wasn't stone too.

"Then up comes young Bill Sublette. He'd been clerkin' down to the fort on the Platte River, so he'd knowed something. He looks and looks, and scrapes the trees with his knife, and snaps the grass like pipestems, and breaks the leaves, a-snappin' 'em like seashells.

" 'What's all this, boy?' I asks.

" 'Putrefactions,' he says, lookin' smart. 'Putrefactions.' "

THE CANYON

This trapper lived in a cabin deep in the mountains at one end of a long box gulch, which is a kind of canyon that after a while runs into a cliff.

Although he lived far from civilization, he had everything he needed. Each night, for example, he would look down the canyon, take a deep breath, and shout:

"Good morning! Good morning!"

Then he would climb into his blanket roll and fall asleep. Seven hours later, to the very minute, the echo of his voice would come booming back.

"GOOD MORNING!
GOOD MORNING!"

he would hear himself shout.

Then he would stretch and yawn and crawl out of bed, ready to start another day.

A CROOKED STREAM

There is a stream near here that twists and turns so often that when you jump across you land on the same side where you started.

The heaviest snow anyone could remember buried every house for miles, including a cabin on a hill at the edge of a deep valley.

After about a week the man who lived in that cabin ran out of firewood and decided he'd better do something about it. So he pulled down some planks from the roof. Then he strapped his snowshoes and an ax to his back and crawled through the roof and the snow to the surface to see what he could find.

But all he could see was the top of one tree, a hickory, about a quarter of a mile away. After he finally reached it, he trimmed its branches, then cut its trunk, which he recalls was at least four feet across.

But as he hauled the tree trunk home, it slipped from his grasp and headed down the hill. Gathering speed, it slid into the valley and up a hill on the other side. There it paused for a minute, then slid back down, then came back up to where he stood waiting to grab it.

But before he could, down it went again, then up it came, then down it went, then up it came, then down it went, as if it had decided never to stop. The man finally gave up and dragged the branches home.

After eight days more, most of the snow had gone. Again he left his cabin. When he looked across the valley this time, he saw a kind of trench between the two hills where that tree trunk had been sliding.

When he followed it, he found at the bottom the trunk, still moving back and forth a little. By now, however, it had worn itself down to the size of a toothpick, like this one.

The man who told me this story wanted me to show it to you so that you would not doubt his word.

6. THE WEATHER

There is one town where the weather is so pleasant and so healthful that nobody ever gets sick. In fact, they had to shoot a man to start a graveyard there.

But most places are not like that.

When the temperature reached 118 degrees a whole field of corn popped. White flakes filled the air and covered the ground six inches deep and drifted across roads and collected on tree limbs.

A mule that saw all this thought it was snowing and lay down and quietly froze to death.

But when the heat popped the corn, it also melted the sugar cane in the next field. And when the cane melted, it oozed through the corn like a giant river and produced enormous balls of popcorn.

The heat was so bad, in fact, the farmer had to feed his hens cracked ice to keep them from laying hard-boiled eggs.

And when his dog chased his cat, they both walked.

It got so cold that winter, this boy's shadow froze right to the side of his house and he had to leave it behind.

The air also froze. And when people spoke, their words froze. One man was strong enough to break the air with his fists, which enabled him to speak. But most people were not that strong.

When this woman tried to call her son, her words froze before they reached him. As a result, he did not come home for two months—not until they finally thawed, and at last he heard her calling.

And when these girls tried to quarrel, they couldn't. Instead of insults, ice cubes tumbled from their mouths, one for each word.

But they were so angry, they collected the ice cubes in sacks and took them home. Then they melted them and listened to their words and enjoyed a good fight.

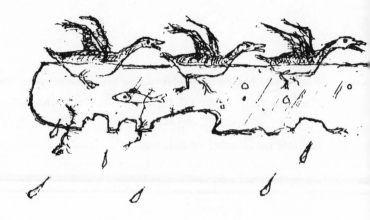

The pond also froze into a solid chunk of ice. It happened so fast that hundreds of ducks that were resting there were trapped. But late that night they flapped their wings so vigorously they flew off with the pond and left nothing behind but a big hole.

Have you heard about the man who crossed a bridge near here in a thick fog? That was the day after it had washed away in a flood. But no one told him.

That same foggy morning a farmer hired a man to shingle the roof of a small barn. It didn't seem like much of a job, but the man didn't come back until dinner time.

When he finally returned, he said, "That's an almighty long barn of your'n."

And the farmer replied, "Not very long."

And the man replied, "Well, I've been at work the whole day, but with the fog and all I am nowhere near finished yet."

And the farmer replied, "Well, you're a lazy fellow. That's all I've got to say."

Then they went down to the meadow to see what he had done. By the time they got there, the fog had lifted a little, so they got a good look. And they both just stood there and stared.

The man had worked hard, all right. He had shingled
a hundred feet of fog along with the barn.

THE RAIN

It rained so hard one day that people had to jump into the river to keep from drowning.

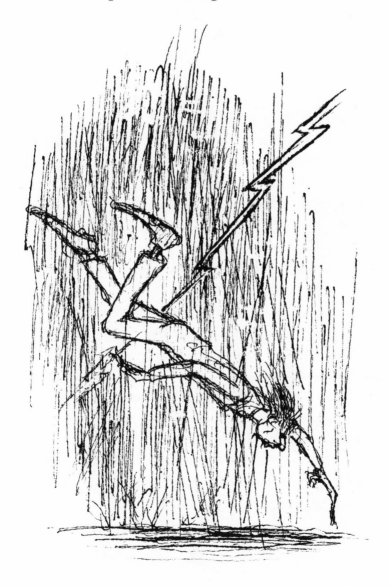

A man riding across the prairie came to the house of a friend who invited him to spend the night. He eagerly accepted, for he had been in the saddle since sunup and still had many miles to go.

Before he took his gear inside, he undid his lariat and tied one end to his horse's halter. Then he tied the other end to a scrub cedar tree about five feet high which was growing out of the top of a small hill.

After dinner a severe windstorm came roaring through. However, the man was so tired he barely noticed and soon was asleep.

But the next morning things didn't look quite the same outside. Instead of a small cedar tree, there now was a large cedar tree at least fifty feet high. And the hill where he had tied his horse was gone. And so was the horse!

But it did not take long to find him. For there he was —dangling from the top of the tree, swinging back and forth a little, but patient as could be, just waiting to be let down.

The man then realized what had happened. When the wind roared through, it blew away the hill, exposed the rest of the tree, and left his horse up in the air.

He climbed up, undid the rope, and gently lowered the horse to the ground. Then he packed his gear and headed for home.

That same storm blew the feathers off a chicken and the chipmunks out of their holes.

It also forced the birds to fly backward to keep the sand out of their eyes.

It also saved a rabbit's life. When a fox came after him, the rabbit put up his ears which caught the wind like a pair of sails. And it blew him away.

But in some places that storm
　did even stranger things.
It blew the cracks out of a fence,
　and the teeth out of a saw,
　and a well out of the ground,
　which the farmer
　then turned upside down
　and used as a silo.
It also moved a township line,
　and changed the time of day
　and the day of the week,
　and kept the sun from setting
　for three hours
　and forty-five minutes.

It also blew the hair off a man's head,
and the whiskers off his face,
and the shoes off his socks,
and the socks off his feet.

Many people who ventured out that day
were blown up against brick walls,
then flattened by the wind
thin as this page,
then peeled off by a businessman
and sold as circus posters.

When that storm was at its worst, one person made the mistake of opening his mouth. Before he knew it, he had swallowed five barrels of air, which blew him up to five times his normal size, which caused him to bounce like a tennis ball.

There is one lie I know I have decided *not* to tell. It is so big a lie it swelled up my left ear when I first heard it. And people came miles to see me fan myself with it. I would not want *that* to happen to you.

Alvin Schwartz

NOTES
SOURCES AND RELATED LIES
BIBLIOGRAPHY
AN ACKNOWLEDGMENT

ABBREVIATIONS IN NOTES, SOURCES, AND BIBLIOGRAPHY

CFQ   *California Folklore Quarterly*
HF   *Hoosier Folklore*
HFB   *Hoosier Folklore Bulletin*
JAF   *Journal of American Folklore*
KFR   *Kentucky Folklore Record*
LC   Library of Congress, Folk Song Section, Washington, D.C. Includes WPA Folklore Archives assembled state by state in the 1930s during the great economic depression. Collectors were unemployed folklorists and writers hired by the federal government.
MF   *Midwest Folklore*
NEFL   *Northeast Folklore*
NYFQ   *New York Folklore Quarterly*
RU   Material from the author's folklore collection, contributed since 1963 by his students at Rutgers University.
SFQ   *Southern Folklore Quarterly*
TXFS   Texas Folklore Society publication
UM   Maryland Folklore Archives, University of Maryland, College Park, Md. Folklore collected by students in 1960s and 1970s.
WF   *Western Folklore*

NOTES

The publications cited are described in the Bibliography.

Tall tales and folk tales. Tall tales are part of a vast body of folk tales which have come down to us over thousands of years by word of mouth and through repeated use in books. These tales are closely related in that their subjects and forms are traditional. But otherwise they differ in many ways.

There are *magic tales* or *fairy tales*, which are concerned with marvels and miracles; *legends,* which describe events said to have occurred at some point in history; *myths,* which deal with gods and other religious figures in the distant past; *hero tales,* which recount the adventures of an individual, usually a superman; *anecdotes,* or brief humorous tales; *animal tales,* which deal with adventures of animals that speak a human tongue and/or have other human traits; and *fables,* which are animal tales that express a moral or lesson.

Most tall tales are either hero tales or anecdotes. A number have characteristics of the magic tale, the legend, or the animal tale. See Thompson, *The Folktale,* pp. 7–10.

Baron Munchausen and "The Turkey Runner." One major source of tall tales was the unknown storyteller who created a tale, then told it to others who passed it on with their imprint. Another major source was writers.

One of the most important of these was Rudolph E. Raspe, the author of a forty-two-page book published in England in 1785. He called it *Baron Munchausen's Narrative of his Marvellous Travels and Campaigns in Russia.* Dr. Raspe was a German professor who fled to England to escape his creditors. Baron Munchausen was Karl Friedrich Hieronymus Freiherr von Münchausen, a German nobleman, adventurer, and storyteller.

Some of the tall tales Raspe reports probably are Munchausen's exaggerations. But most were taken from lying tales told by German monks for their amusement, and from other early sources. The book quickly became a best-seller. It then was expanded by various teams of writers and reprinted in edition after edition.

It also was translated into many tongues. In 1862, seventy-seven years after "the Baron" first appeared, the famous French writer Théophile Gautier brought out an expanded edition of his own. Only a few years ago a new American edition appeared. See Carswell, *Singular Travels, Campaigns and Adventures of Baron Munchausen.*

A half dozen of the tales in *Whoppers* are descended from Munchausen material; these are noted in the Sources.

Another important body of tall tales was created in the years before the Civil War by a large group of American editors, lawyers, politicians (including congressmen), doctors, actors, ships' captains, and other professionals. Writing for their own pleasure, they reported on amusing and curious happenings in the South and Southwest which they encountered in day-to-day life, then embellished.

Much of their work was published in weekly newspapers. The most important of these was a sporting newspaper with a national circulation, the New York *Spirit of the Times, a Chronicle of the Turf, Agriculture, Field Sports, Literature, and the Stage.* Its editor, William T. Porter, was one of the nation's great journalists.

It was the *Spirit* that published "Chunkey's Fight with the Panters" (p. 66), the work of an anonymous writer who called himself "The Turkey Runner." It also published "The Big Bear of Arkansas," by Thomas Bangs Thorpe, one of the great American tall stories.

Since newspapers in that period stole freely from one another, good tall tales received wide circulation. The best of this material also was collected in books which survive today in research libraries as important tall tale collections. See Porter, *The Big Bear of Arkansas* and *A Quarter Race in Kentucky,* and Longstreet, *Georgia Scenes.* For a discussion of the literary tall tale in the United States see Chittick, *Ring-Tailed Roarers,* and Meine, *Tall Tales from the Southwest.*

Heroes. The tall tales in *Whoppers* involve ordinary people.

But the best-known American tall tales deal, of course, with individuals who performed superhuman feats, around whom cycles of tales developed. Among these "supermen" are three types it is useful to recognize.

1. Real persons who became larger than life through tales they told about themselves and others told about them. In the process they achieved the status of authentic folk heroes. These include national heroes like Davy Crockett, the adventurer and politician; Mike Fink, the Mississippi River boatman; Jim Bridger, the Rocky Mountain scout; and regional heroes like John Darling of New York, "Oregon" Smith of Indiana, and Big-Foot Wallace of Texas.

2. Fictitious folk heroes who emerged from the characteristics and experiences of occupational, ethnic, and racial groups whose lives were beset by hardship and who needed a heroic figure as inspiration. Stormalong, the hero of old deep-water sailors, was one such character. John Henry, the black laborer whose legendary strength inspired a famous ballad, was another.

3. "Heroes" who are believed to have few roots, if any, in folklore. They include the logger Paul Bunyan, the Texas cowboy Pecos Bill, the Nebraska farmer Febold Feboldson, and the steel worker from Pittsburgh, Joe Magarac.

Bunyan's situation is the most complicated. Some researchers say he probably was a minor legendary figure who developed in the 1830s among French-Canadian loggers. But folklorists find most woodsmen know little about him other than what they have read.

It was not until the early 1900s, in fact, that Paul Bunyan achieved a degree of fame. That happened when the Red River Lumber Company in Minnesota began to use his name and likeness in advertisements and prepared a series of booklets which contained tales about his feats.

W. B. Laughhead, who wrote and illustrated the first of these booklets, claims to have invented Babe the Blue Ox, Johnny Inkslinger, Sourdough Sam, and other familiar characters.

Pecos Bill first appeared in 1923 in an article by Edward O'Reilly in *Century Magazine*. Febold Feboldson was created for advertising purposes the same year by a lumber dealer in Gothenburg, Nebraska. Joe Magarac was created in 1930 to help humanize the United States Steel Corporation.

Almost all the tales that exist today about these characters, including Bunyan, were created by writers for young people. Many are good stories, but they do not classify as folklore, for they do not arise out of human needs and experience. The folklorist Richard M. Dorson calls such material "fakelore." See Dorson, *America in Legend*, pp. 168–170; Thompson, *The Folktale*, p. 250; *Standard Dictionary*, v. 2, pp. 847–848. Also see entries in the Bibliography regarding folk heroes.

Holman F. Day (p. 3): Unlike traditional folklorists, Day did not produce word for word the tall tales and other tales he collected in Maine at the turn of the century. Instead, he turned them into amusing ballads which fill three volumes. For examples, see p. 3, pp. 32–33, and on p. 110, the note for p. 18.

Tall talk (p. 30): When Bob jumped into the air, cracked his heels together and shouted, "I'm the old original iron-jawed, brass-mounted, copper-bellied corpse-maker," he was using tall talk. When others used words like "rumfuzzled" for confused and frustrated, "slantidicular" for slantwise, "rumbinate" for think, and "tetotactiously exfluncated" for totally beat, they also were using tall talk.

With its bold, boisterous language, often with exaggeration heaped upon exaggeration, tall talk was used in the backwoods and on the frontier for the same reasons tall tales were. It was fun, and it made the users feel better. See Boatright, *Folk Laughter on the American Frontier*, pp. 146–158.

Hunting tales (p. 39): Since the backwoodsman and the frontiersman once counted on hunting for food, probably the largest number of American tall tales are concerned with this activity. The tale of Ab Yancey's lucky shot is repeated in countless forms in American folklore. Three other themes also occur again and again:

The bent gun: A hunter finds a flock of birds perched around the edge of a pond. To kill them, he bends the barrel of his rifle so that it corresponds to the curve of the shoreline. Then he fires and hits every one. In some versions, he forgets to get out of the way of the returning bullet and is hit, but usually he survives because by then the force of the bullet is spent. See Packard, *Old Plymouth Trails*, pp. 204–206.

Slow powder: A hunter finds that his gun or his powder is not powerful enough to propel a bullet with sufficient force to do the job. He therefore runs alongside the bullet and pats it to keep it moving and on target. In a Maine version, the hunter uses a canoe paddle. See Lunt, *NEFL* 10, p. 38.

Split bullet: Usually the hunter has only one bullet left but sees two birds or animals, one on either side of a pointed rock. He aims for the point, which splits the bullet, whose parts kill both targets.

Frozen death (p. 62): There is a detective story here. The freezing and thawing supposedly took place in the 1880s in a mountain hamlet in Vermont within twenty-five miles of Montpelier. But the events actually took place only in the mind of a farmer named Allen Morse who in 1887 wrote an article on the subject he signed A.M. and sent to the Montpelier newspaper. The paper published the article, but if anyone took the hoax seriously it soon was forgotten.

In 1939, however, the article turned up in an old scrapbook owned by a man named Elbert S. Stevens. It then was reprinted in the *Rutland Herald* in Vermont and in the *Boston Globe*.

The following year *Yankee* magazine published a story about the freezing and thawing, and the year after that Charles E. Crane devoted a chapter to the subject in his book *Winter in Vermont*. In 1943 the *Old Farmer's Almanac* gave the details. In 1946 *Yankee* repeated the story. And in 1949 *Vermont Life*, another magazine, also ran an article.

This one produced an avalanche of letters—including one from Florida, from Allen Morse's granddaughter, who told what had happened. After sixty-two years the game was up. But Allen Morse was indeed a hard liar.

See Botkin, *A Treasury of New England Folklore*, pp. 164–168; Dorson, *Jonathan Draws the Long Bow*, p. 23; Crane, p. 85.

SOURCES AND RELATED LIES

The source of each item is given, along with significant variants. Where available, the names of collectors (C) and informants (I) are provided. The publications cited are described in full in the Bibliography. The term "general" indicates that the item is widespread and has been retold by the author.

p. 3   *'Twould make an ox:* Excerpted from "Zek'l Pratt's Harrycane" in Day, *Up in Maine,* p. 89. See note to p. 3, "Holman F. Day."

1.

ORDINARY PEOPLE

p. 15   *So small:* Adapted from *Yankee Notions,* Boston, 8 (1858), p. 138, as quoted in Loomis, *WF* 6, p. 214. VARI-ANTS: A man so small it takes two men to see him, Kempt, *The American Joe Miller,* p. 71; two men and a boy, Sandburg, *The People, Yes,* p. 89.

p. 16   *So fast:* General.

p. 18   *So tall:* Adapted from *Turner's Comic Almanack,* 1843, as quoted in Botkin, *A Treasury of New England Folklore,* p. 130. *Feet so big:* General. *So nimble:* A feat described in the *Daily Evening Transcript,* Boston (August 27, 1835), and in "Grampy's Lullabye," Day, *Up in Maine,* pp. 23–24. In the latter, Ebenezer Cowles "skittered up that larder 'fore she had a chance to teeter/Quicker'n any pussy cat—lighter'n a moskeeter."

p. 19   *So strong: Golden Era,* San Francisco, 17 (1869), no. 6, p. 7. *Rock juice:* Author's lie. *Breaks boulders:* Quarry workers in one Illinois county are said to perform this feat. Jack Conroy, "The Sissy from Hardscrabble County Rock Quarries," LC, Illinois, 1937. *Squeezes pieces:* Calvin Corey, a New York State logger, claimed to have done this. "After that they knew what kind of a feller I was," he said. Thompson, *Body, Boots & Britches,* p. 145.

p. 20   *Pulling crooked roads straight:* A feat attributed to Joe

Mouffreau, a French-Canadian logger said to have been seven feet tall. He used a yoke of oxen and a chain so heavy it took ten men to carry it. Reported by Dorson, *America in Legend*, p. 175.

p. 21 *So stingy:* General. *So tenderhearted:* General.

2.

ORDINARY THINGS

p. 22 *Cucumbers:* General. For texts, see Randolph, *We Always Lie to Strangers*, p. 83; Arrowood, TXFS 18, pp. 83–84. VARIANTS: Farmer cuts himself loose, but finds a cucumber gone to seed in one of his pockets, Kempt, *The American Joe Miller*, p. 149; farmer is saved by father from pumpkin vines, Federal Writers' Project, *Hoosier Tall Stories*, pp. 26–27.

p. 23 *Corn:* General. For texts, see Randolph, *We Always Lie to Strangers*, p. 77; Halpert, *HF* 7, p. 69; Welsch, *Shingling the Fog*, p. 60; Smith, *MF* 1, p. 93. In the Smith version a man drops seed corn which springs up behind him and carries him skyward. In a related tale a stalk of corn grows so rapidly it leaves the ground and takes its roots with it, general.

p. 26 *Raise . . . a fuss:* General. VARIANT: Two red-headed women couldn't raise a ruckus, Randolph, *We Always Lie to Strangers*, p. 24. *Pancakes:* Adapted from Sandburg, *The People, Yes*, p. 88. *Chickens:* Adapted from Welsch, *Shingling the Fog*, p. 100.

p. 27 *Fiddle:* Adapted from *Spirit of the Times*, New York, 2 (June, 1860), p. 18, as quoted in Loomis, *WF* 6, p. 36. *These two old-timers:* General. For texts, see Federal Writers' Project, *Hoosier Tall Stories*, pp. 15–16; Dobie, *Vanity Fair*, March, 1932, p. 32; Thompson, *Body, Boots & Britches*, p. 141. Thompson reports a duel in which one participant's bullet enters the other's gun barrel and plugs it.

p. 30 *Bob and the Child of Calamity:* Clemens, *Life on the Mississippi*, pp. 18–20. Adapted. See note to p. 30, "Tall talk."

p. 32 *The Spang-Fired Truth:* Excerpted and adapted from the ballad "Grampy Sings a Song," Day, *Up in Maine*, pp. 80–82.

p. 34 *Nine years ago:* One of the many versions of a classic American fish story. This account is adapted from *The Tame Trout and Other Fairy Tales* as quoted in Farquhar, *CFQ* 3, pp. 177–179. For a similar account, see Goodspeed, *Angling in America*, pp. 315–316. VARIANTS: A baby turtle is adopted by a cat, but cannot follow its new "parent" up a tree during a flood and drowns, Smith, *MF* 1, p. 96.

p. 35 *Such a big fish:* General.

p. 36 *Billie the Dolphin:* LC, Chicago, Illinois, 1936. Adapted from text of an unedited interview, C: Jack Conroy, I: Charlie DeMelo.

p. 39 *Ab Yancey tells it:* Randolph, *Ozark Mountain Folks*, pp. 143–145. Adapted. See note to p. 39, "Hunting tales."

p. 42 **This artist.** *Dog:* Author's lie. *Snowstorm:* Kempt, *The American Joe Miller*, p. 71. VARIANT: An artist who painted a cannon so naturally that it went off when he finished, *Spirit of the Times*, New York, 3 (1860), p. 23, as quoted in Loomis, *WF* 6, p. 222.

p. 43 *Prospecting for silver:* Adapted from *Colorado Miner*, Denver, January 24, 1880, p. 1. For a complete text, see Botkin, *A Treasury of Western Folklore*, pp. 439–440. *Pulling teeth: The Crockett Almanac*, 1841, p. 19. Adapted.

3.

FANCY CLOTHES
AND NARROW ESCAPES

p. 46 *Where Joe Merriweather Went To: Spirit of the Times*, New York, February 8, 1851. Excerpted and adapted from a longer tale. For a complete text, see Chittick, *Ring-Tailed Roarers*, pp. 41–45; Rourke, *American Humor*, pp. 46–48.

p. 49 *Inside out:* General. Based on a Munchausen theme. VARI-

ANTS: Hunter pulls tongue instead of tail, LC, Indiana, 1939. Bear is white on the inside, Lunt, *NEFL* 10, p. 44. In other accounts, a cougar or panther is turned inside out.

p. 50 *Raspberries:* General. For texts, see Federal Writers' Project, *Hoosier Tall Stories,* p. 8; Randolph, *We Always Lie to Strangers,* p. 268; Halpert, *HF* 7, p. 69.

p. 51 *Oliver Stanley is Kidnumped:* Taliaferro, *Fisher's River* (*North Carolina*), pp. 133–138. Adapted.

p. 54 *The Trap:* General. For texts, see Boatright, *Tall Tales from Texas Cow Camps,* pp. 59–64; Welsch, *Shingling the Fog,* p. 50. VARIANTS: Wild geese carry off a hunter after he tries to trap them by tying them together, LC, Union County, Arkansas, 1936, C: Carol Graham. Wild turkeys carry off an Ozark hunter when he grabs them by the legs, Randolph, *We Always Lie to Strangers,* pp. 122–123. Variants of theme in which a victim frees himself: A horse falls on his rider's foot; the rider then walks twelve miles for a pole to pry off the horse, Halpert, *CFQ* 4, p. 251. A tree falls on a hunter who goes for an ax to cut himself loose, Halpert *et al., HFB* 1, pp. 91–92. This theme also is reported in Munchausen.

p. 56 *Halfway:* Belmont School, Philadelphia, 1972; Dirks, *WF* 22, p. 100. VARIANTS: A man leaps the width of a river, then whirls and without descending returns to where he started, Sandburg, *The People, Yes,* p. 91. *Boots:* Excerpted and adapted from Carter, *A Summer Cruise on the Coast of New England,* pp. 106–108. For a complete text, see Dorson, *Jonathan Draws the Long Bow,* pp. 108–110. VARIANT: A rattlesnake's fangs are imbedded in a leather boot after the snake strikes and kills the boot's owner. Persons who subsequently inherit the boots die from contact with the fangs before the fangs are discovered, Masterson, *Tall Tales of Arkansas,* pp. 390–393; Benton, *An Artist in America,* pp. 210–211; Boatright, *Tall Tales from Texas Cow Camps,* pp. 52–54.

p. 60 *Uncle Davy Lane Loses His Underwear:* Taliaferro, *Fisher's River* (*North Carolina*), pp. 52–55. Adapted.

p. 62   *Frozen Death:* Wilson, *The Old Farmer's Almanac,* 1943, pp. 50, 83. Adapted. See note to p. 62, "Frozen Death."

p. 66   *Chunkey's Fight with the Panters:* Adapted from *Spirit of the Times,* New York, May 18, 1844, as quoted in Chittick, *Ring-Tailed Roarers,* pp. 130–137, which provides a complete text.

p. 70   *Jim Got Murdered: Spirit of the Times,* New York, 16 (April 18, 1846), p. 85. "Jim" was Jim Mussett, better known to readers of the *Spirit of the Times* and other pre–Civil War publications as "Old Sense," a braggart and adventurer created by C. F. M. Noland.

4.

ANIMALS AND INSECTS

p. 71   *Cats:* LC, Old Town, Maine, 1939, I: Mike Pelletier. Adapted. VARIANT: This cat hid near a rat hole, made sounds like a piece of cheese, then hit the rats over the head as they came out in search of food, Halpert and Holaday, *HFB* 2, p. 63.

p. 73   *Dogs:* Adapted from Taliaferro, *Fisher's River* (*North Carolina*), pp. 149–151. Based on a Munchausen theme. The reference to barking out of both ends is borrowed from an account in Chase, *American Folk Tales and Songs,* p. 98. VARIANTS: A dog splits itself on a wire, Cardwell, *KFR* 6, p. 44; a moving saw, *Yankee Notions,* Boston, 8 (1858), p. 262, as quoted in Loomis, *WF* 6, p. 33; a sapling, Smith, *MF* 1, p. 97. Tar is used to stick the dog together Gates, *TXFS* 14, p. 264. In other accounts the split animal is a fox or a panther.

p. 75   **Hogs.** *So thin:* General. VARIANT: Several must stand in the same place to cast a shadow, general. *So weak:* S. S. Cox, *Why We Laugh* (New York, 1871), p. 88, as quoted in Boatright, *Laughter on the American Frontier,* p. 81.

p. 76   *Mosquitoes are so big:* General. The numbers required to subdue various creatures vary widely.

p. 77   **Mosquitoes.** *Fly off with pot:* General. VARIANTS: The pot is a kettle, a sap kettle in a maple sugar camp, an iron tank, and a tent, among other things. For texts, see Halpert, *CFQ* 4, p. 45; Randolph, *We Always Lie to Strangers*, p. 147; Davidson, *Rocky Mountain Tales*, p. 280; Lunt, *NEFL* 10, p. 25. *The big guys will grab him:* General. For texts, Randolph, citing old press reports in *We Always Lie to Strangers*, p. 149; Welsch, *Shingling the Fog*, p. 112; Federal Writers' Project, *Idaho Lore*, p. 138; Halpert *et al.*, *HFB* 1, pp. 93–94; LC, Bloomington, Indiana, 1938, C: E. R. Dodson, I: Earl Boyer.

p. 78   *The largest mosquito ever seen:* LC, Illinois, 1937, C: Mary Mears, I: Edith Driscoll.

    RELATED LIES: A group that involves grasshoppers who are so hungry, or so large, or both, they eat stone fences, horses, and cows; steal lunches from children on their way to school; and when captured help with the plowing, general.

p. 80   **Snakes.** *Swallowed each other:* General. For texts, see Boatright, *Tall Tales from Texas Cow Camps*, p. 11; Lunt, *NEFL* 10, p. 43. VARIANT: A snake swallows itself, Sandburg, *The People, Yes*, p. 89. A frog and a snake swallow each other, *Spirit of the Times*, New York, 1860, p. 151. *Grateful snake:* General. This version adapted from LC, Marion County, Indiana, 1938. For other texts, see Federal Writers' Project, *Idaho Lore*, p. 116; Davidson, *SFQ* 5, p. 205; Davidson, *Rocky Mountain Tales*, p. 268; *Nebraska Farmer*, February 27, 1925, as quoted in Welsch, *Shingling the Fog*, p. 96. VARIANTS: A man caught a snake so friendly it permitted itself to be used as a clothesline, Sutherland, *Tall Tales of the Devil's Apron*, p. 84. A United States Marine frees from under a rock a rattlesnake which becomes his companion for a period. At a later time the Marine encounters a snake he is about to kill when it identifies itself through a message it rattles in Morse code, Davidson, *Tales They Tell in the Services*, p. 53.

p. 81   *Spiders:* Duval, *Adventures of Big-Foot Wallace*, p. 276. Adapted.

5.

PUTREFACTIONS
AND OTHER WONDERS

p. 82   *A Putrified Forest:* Ruxton, *Life in the Far West,* pp. 16–
17. Adapted. VARIANTS: Petrified gravity, Carmer, *The
Hurricane's Children,* p. 58. A petrified Indian, Arrowood,
TXFS 18, p. 84; Jim Bridger's report on peetrifaction,
J. Cecil Alter, *James Bridger, Trapper, Frontiersman,
Scout and Guide* (Columbus, Ohio, 1951) as quoted in
Botkin, *A Treasury of Western Folklore,* p. 643.

p. 83   *The Canyon:* General. VARIANT: The "alarm" calls "Time
to git up!," general.

p. 84   *A Crooked Stream: Boston Herald,* February 5, 1858, as
quoted in Loomis, *WF* 6, p. 38. Adapted.

p. 85   *A Hickory Tree:* A retelling of a tale heard at children's
camps in New York and New Hampshire. For other texts,
see MacKaye, *Tall Tales of the Kentucky Mountains,* pp.
67–68; Chase, *American Folk Tales and Songs,* pp. 98–100.

6.

THE WEATHER

p. 87   *The weather is so healthful:* Boatright, *Folk Laughter on
the American Frontier,* p. 83; *Spirit of the Times,* New
York, 2 (June, 1860), p. 170, as quoted in Loomis, *WF* 6,
p. 225. VARIANT: The climate is so healthful that people
do not die; they dry up and blow away, *Yankee Notions,*
Boston, 3 (1854), p. 354, as quoted in Loomis, *WF* 6, p.
225.

p. 88   *A mule froze to death:* General. This version adapted from
LC, Hillsdale, Indiana, 1938, C: Eva Nelson, I: Ezra
Hunt. VARIANTS: The mule is nearsighted, the animal is a
horse, several animals are affected simultaneously, general. The victim is a loafer who is asleep when the corn
pops. He awakens, thinks it is snowing, and freezes to
death, for he is too lazy to move, LC, Indiana Jokes–
Hyperbole, 1938.

p. 89   *Cracked ice:* Robinson, *Yarns of the Southwest,* p. 17. *Dog chased cat:* General.

p. 90   *Shadow froze:* General. *Air froze:* General. *Words froze:* General. *Strong enough to break air:* Thompson, *Body, Boots & Britches,* p. 138.

p. 91   *Woman tried to call son:* General. Related to Munchausen tale of tunes that froze in the posthorn, then played in order when the horn was thawed, and to sixteenth-century Italian tale. *Girls tried to quarrel:* Author's lie. VARIANTS: A foreman on a ranch gives instructions to his men, then breaks off the frozen words as he speaks and hands them out, Halpert, *CFQ* 4, p. 43. Words are caught in a sack, then taken home and thawed, Welsch, *Shingling the Fog,* p. 28. Frying pans are used to catch frozen words, Fauset, *JAF* 40, p. 261. In a group of related tales and lies, fire freezes.

p. 92   *The pond froze:* General. VARIANTS: Ducks caught in ice fly off with pond when hunter fires at them, LC, Chattanooga, Tennessee, 1937, C: Eugene Dervieux, I: Rosa Toung. Birds caught in frozen lake fly off with it, leaving the Grand Canyon, Halpert *et al., HFB* 1, p. 93. A flock of crows flies off with a barn roof after a farmer runs out of ammunition and fires carpet tacks at them; the tacks nail their feet fast, Larson, *NYFQ* 18, p. 220.

p. 93   **Fog.** *Crossed a bridge:* Deer Isle, Maine. *Shingling the fog:* General. This version is adapted from Kempt, *The American Joe Miller,* pp. 57–58. VARIANTS: Many involving how far beyond roof the shingler goes, and whether he moves off to the left or right or up from the ridge pole.

p. 95   *The rain: Yankee Notions,* Boston, 12 (1853), p. 125, as quoted in Loomis, *WF* 6, p. 225.

p. 96   *The hanging horse:* General. This version is adapted from LC, New Mexico, 1937, C: W. M. Emery. VARIANTS: In a Munchausen tale, a horse tethered to a post during a blizzard is found the next morning, after the snow has melted, hanging from a church steeple. A tree is buried in deep snow which melts, leaving horse high and dry, Halpert, *CFQ* 4, p. 37. A tree limb springs up, and with it a horse tethered to it, when a flock of pigeons roosting on the limb fly away, Taliaferro, *Fisher's River* (*North Carolina*), pp. 79–84. For similar tale see "The Springing Tree," *Daily Evening Transcript*, Boston, July 16, 1835, as quoted in Loomis, *WF* 6, pp. 37–38.

p. 98   *Feathers:* General. *Chipmunks:* General. VARIANT: In some lies squirrels are the victims.

p. 99   *Birds:* Barton, TXFS 14, p. 266. *Rabbit blew away:* Belmont School, Philadelphia, 1972. A similar lie is reported by Botkin, *A Treasury of American Folklore*, p. 513. *Blew cracks out of a fence:* LC, Nebraska, 1939. *Teeth out of a saw:* Thompson, *Body, Boots & Britches*, p. 138. *Well out of the ground:* General. VARIANTS: Oil gushed from hole left by well, making farmer wealthy, *The Prairie Schooner*, April, 1927, p. 158, as quoted by Welsch, *Shingling the Fog*, p. 24. A dry well blown out of the ground was cut into holes for fence posts, general. *Moved a township line:* LC, Nebraska, 1939. *Changed time of day:* General. *Changed day of week:* LC, Nebraska, 1939. *Kept sun from setting:* General. This version is adapted from LC, Oklahoma, 1937. VARIANT: Took until after midnight to set, *Missouri College Farmer*, January, 1947, as quoted in Randolph, *We Always Lie to Strangers*, p. 193.

p. 100   *Blew hair off:* General. *Blew whiskers off:* Author's lie. VARIANT: In a high wind a ship's sailors held the captain's beard in place, Kempt, *The American Joe Miller*, p. 71. *Blew shoes off:* Author's lie. *Blew socks off: The Nebraska Farmer*, March 14, 1925, as quoted in Welsch, *Shingling the Fog*, p. 22. *Flattened thin:* Perkins, *Library of Wit and Humor*, p. 216. Adapted. VARIANT: A woman driven against a cliff by the wind is flattened to a thickness of two inches and can eat nothing but corn fritters and skimmed milk for a week, Sutherland, *Tall Tales of the Devil's Apron*, p. 221.

p. 101   *Opening his mouth:* RU, 1973. A similar tale is reported in Koch, *Kansas Folklore*, p. 109.

p. 102   *There is one lie:* Parts of this reference to a monstrous falsehood swelling the author's ear are borrowed from Clemens, *Life on the Mississippi*, p. 260.

BIBLIOGRAPHY

The publications cited offer historical and technical background, explore traditional tall tale motifs, and provide examples and analysis of hero tales and literary tall tales.

Books that may be of particular interest to young people are marked with an asterisk (*). Major collections are marked with a dagger (†).

BOOKS

Adventures of Baron Munchausen, The. New York: Pantheon Books, 1969.

† Beath, Paul, and Trank, Lynn. *Febold Feboldson: Tall Tales from the Great Plains.* Lincoln, Neb.: University of Nebraska Press, 1948.

Benton, Thomas Hart. *An Artist in America.* 3d ed. Columbia, Mo.: University of Missouri Press, 1968.

† Blair, Walter. *Native American Humor (1800–1900).* New York: American Book Co., 1937. Reprint edition, San Francisco: Chandler Publishing Company, 1960.

* ———. *Tall Tale America: A Legendary History of Our Humorous Heroes.* New York: Coward-McCann, Inc., 1944.

———, and Meine, Franklin J., eds. *Half Horse, Half Alligator: The Growth of the Mike Fink Legend.* Chicago: University of Chicago Press, 1956.

Boatright, Mody C. *Folk Laughter on the American Frontier.* New York: Macmillan Company, 1949.

†* ———. *Tall Tales from Texas Cow Camps.* Dallas: Southwest Press, 1934.

†* Botkin, B. A., ed. *A Treasury of American Folklore.* New York: Crown Publishers, Inc., 1944.

†* ———, ed. *A Treasury of New England Folklore.* New York: Crown Publishers, Inc., 1965.

†* ———, ed. *A Treasury of Western Folklore.* New York: Crown Publishers, Inc., 1951.

* Bowman, James C. *Pecos Bill*. Chicago: Albert Whitman & Co., 1937.

* Carmer, Carl L. *The Hurricane's Children: Tales from Your Neck o' the Woods*. New York and Toronto: Farrar & Rinehart, 1937.

Carswell, John, ed. *Singular Travels, Campaigns and Adventures of Baron Munchausen, by R. E. Raspe and Others*. London: Cresset Press, 1948.

Carter, Robert. *A Summer Cruise on the Coast of New England*. Boston: Crosby & Nichols, 1864.

* Chase, Richard, ed. *American Folk Tales and Songs*. New York: New American Library, 1956. Reprint edition, New York: Dover Publications, 1971.

†* ———, ed. *Jack Tales*. Boston: Houghton Mifflin Co., 1943.

† Chittick, V. L. O., ed. *Ring-Tailed Roarers: Tall Tales of the American Frontier 1830–60*. Caldwell, Idaho: Caxton Printers, Ltd., 1941.

* Clemens, Samuel L. [Mark Twain]. *Life on the Mississippi*. Boston: J. R. Osgood and Company, 1883. Reprint edition, New York and London: Harper & Brothers, Publishers, 1904.

Crane, Charles F. *Winter in Vermont*. New York: Alfred A. Knopf, 1941.

Crockett Almanac, The. Boston: J. Fisher, 1841.

* Daugherty, James. *Their Weight in Wild Cats*. Boston: Houghton Mifflin Co., 1936.

Davidson, Bill. *Tales They Tell in the Services*. New York: Thomas Y. Crowell Co., 1943.

* Davidson, Levette J., and Blake, Forrester, eds. *Rocky Mountain Tales*. Norman, Okla.: University of Oklahoma Press, 1947.

†* Day, Holman F. *Up in Maine*. Boston: Small, Maynard & Co., 1901. *See note to p. 3*, "Holman F. Day."

Dorson, Richard M. *America in Legend, Folklore from the Colonial Period to the Present*. New York: Pantheon Books, 1973. *A survey*.

† ———. *Buying the Wind: Regional Folklore in the United States*. Chicago and London: University of Chicago Press, 1964.

† ———, ed. *Davy Crockett, American Comic Legend.* New York: Rockland Editions, 1939.

† ———. *Jonathan Draws the Long Bow.* Cambridge, Mass.: Harvard University Press, 1946. Reprint edition, New York: Russell & Russell, 1969. *A study of the folk tale in New England.*

* Duval, John C. *Adventures of Big-Foot Wallace, the Texas Ranger and Hunter.* Philadelphia: Claxton, Remsen & Haffelfinger, 1871.

Federal Writers' Project. *Hoosier Tall Stories.* Washington, D.C.: Works Progress Administration, 1939.

* ———. *Idaho Lore.* Caldwell, Idaho: Caxton Printers, Ltd., 1939.

* Felton, Harold W. *John Henry and His Hammer.* New York: Alfred A. Knopf, 1950.

Goodspeed, Charles E. *Angling in America.* Boston: Houghton Mifflin Co., 1939.

* Jagendorf, Moritz A. *The Marvelous Adventures of Johnny Darling.* New York: Vanguard Press, 1949.

Kempt, Robert, ed. *The American Joe Miller: A Collection of Yankee Wit and Humor.* London: Adams and Francis, 1865.

Koch, William E., and Sackett, Sidney J. *Kansas Folklore.* Lincoln, Neb.: University of Nebraska Press, 1961.

* Leach, Maria. *The Rainbow Book of American Folk Tales and Legends.* Cleveland and New York: World Publishing Company, 1958.

† Longstreet, Augustus B. *Georgia Scenes.* New York: Harper & Brothers, 1835. *A classic collection of early Southern and Southwestern frontier humor.*

† MacKaye, Percy. *Tall Tales of the Kentucky Mountains.* New York: George H. Doran Company, 1926.

* Malcomson, Anne. *Yankee Doodle's Cousins.* Boston: Houghton Mifflin Co., 1941.

† Masterson, James R. *Tall Tales of Arkansas.* Boston: Chapman & Grimes, 1942.

Meine, Franklin J., ed. *The Crockett Almanacs.* Chicago: Caxton Club, 1955.

† ———, ed. *Tall Tales from the Southwest: An Anthology of*

Southern and Southwestern Humor. New York: Alfred A. Knopf, 1930.

Packard, Winthrop. *Old Plymouth Trails.* Boston: Small, Maynard & Co., 1920.

Perkins, Eli [Melville D. Landon]. *Library of Wit and Humor by Mark Twain and Others, with the Philosophy of Wit and Humor.* Chicago: Thompson & Thomas, 1898.

† Porter, William T., ed. *The Big Bear of Arkansas, and Other Sketches.* Philadelphia: Cary and Hart, 1845. *A Collection of tall tales and lies from the* Spirit of the Times, *a humorous sporting weekly Porter edited from 1831 to 1858.*

† ———, ed. *A Quarter Race in Kentucky, and Other Sketches.* Philadelphia: Cary & Hart, 1847.

Price, Robert. *Johnny Appleseed, Man and Myth.* Bloomington, Ind.: Indiana University Press, 1954.

Randolph, Vance. *Ozark Mountain Folks.* New York: Vanguard Press, 1932.

† ———. *We Always Lie to Strangers: Tall Tales from the Ozarks.* New York: Columbia University Press, 1951.

Robinson, Will H. *Yarns of the Southwest.* Phoenix, Ariz.: Berryhill Company, 1921.

Root, Frank A., and Connelly, William E. *The Overland Stage to California.* Topeka, Kan.: published by authors, 1901.

* Rounds, Glen. *Ol' Paul: The Mighty Logger.* New York: Holiday House, 1936.

Rourke, Constance. *American Humor: A Study of the National Character.* Harcourt, Brace & Company, 1931. Reprint edition, New York: Harcourt, Brace, Jovanovitch, Inc., Harvest Books, 1959. *A seminal study of the roots of American humor.*

Russell, Charles M. *Trails Plowed Under.* Garden City, N.Y.: Doubleday, Doran & Co., 1940.

Ruxton, George Frederic. *Life in the Far West.* New York: Harper & Brothers, 1849.

* Sandburg, Carl. *The People, Yes.* New York: Harcourt, Brace & Company, 1936. *See the segment "They have yarns . . ." for a summary of American tall tale motifs.*

* Shapiro, Irwin. *Heroes in American Folklore.* New York: Julian Messner, 1962.

†* Shepherd, Esther. *Paul Bunyan.* New York: Harcourt, Brace & Company, 1925.

Skinner, Charles M. *American Myths and Legends.* 2 vols. Philadelphia and London: J. B. Lippincott Company, 1903.

Standard Dictionary of Folklore, Mythology, and Legend. Edited by Maria Leach. 2 vols. New York: Funk & Wagnalls, Inc., 1949.

* Stoutenburg, Adrien. *American Tall Tales.* New York: Viking Press, 1966.

Sutherland, Herbert M., *Tall Tales of the Devil's Apron.* Radford, Va.: Commonwealth Press, 1970. *Virginia tall tales.*

Taliaferro, H. E. ["Skitt"]. *Fisher's River (North Carolina): Scenes and Characters.* New York: Harper & Brothers, 1859. *Based on material recalled by the author from the 1820s, this is one of the oldest American tall tale collections.*

Thomas, Lowell. *Tall Stories: The Rise and Triumph of the Great American Whopper.* New York and London: Funk & Wagnalls Company, 1931.

† Thompson, Harold W. *Body, Boots & Britches.* Philadelphia: J. B. Lippincott Company, 1940. *New York tall tales.*

Thompson, Stith. *The Folktale.* New York: Holt, Rinehart & Winston, 1946. *A seminal work.*

Tidwell, James N., ed. *A Treasury of American Folk Humor.* New York: Crown Publishers, Inc., 1956.

Welsch, Roger. *Shingling the Fog and Other Plains Tales: Tall Tales of the Great Plains.* Chicago: The Swallow Press, 1972.

ARTICLES

Arrowood, Charles F. "Well Done, Liar." TXFS 18 (1943):79–88.

Ashabranner, Brent. "Pecos Bill—An Appraisal." WF 11 (1952): 20–24.

Barton, Henry W. "Sand Storm Yarns." TXFS 14 (1938):266–267.

† Boggs, Ralph Steele, ed. "North Carolina Folktales Current in the 1820's." JAF 47 (1934):270–288. *Analysis, with representa-*

tive material, of Taliaferro, Fisher's River (North Carolina); see section "Books."

Cardwell, Alma, *et al.* "Tall Tales." *KFR* 6 (1960):42–45.

Davidson, Levette J. "Rocky Mountain Folklore." *SFQ* 5 (1941): 205–219.

Deaver, J. M. "Fishback Yarns from the Sulphurs." TXFS 7 (1928):42–44.

† Dirks, Martha. "Teen-Age Folklore from Kansas." *WF* 22 (1963):89–102.

Dobie, J. Frank. "Great Liars of the Golden West." *Vanity Fair* (1932):31–32, 74.

Farquhar, Samuel T. "The Tame Trout." *CFQ* 3 (1944):177–184. Quoting a 24-page pamphlet, *The Tame Trout and Other Fairy Tales.* Narrated by Ed Grant of Beaver Pond, Maine. Chronicled by Francis I. Maule of Philadelphia. Phillips: Maine Woods and Woodsman Print, 1904.

† Fauset, Arthur Huff. "Negro Folk Tales from the South." *JAF* 40 (1927):213–303.

Gates, Sue. "Windy Yesterdays." TXFS 14 (1938):264–265.

Halpert, Herbert. "Aggressive Humor on the East Branch." *NYFQ* 2 (1946):85–97.

———. "Folktales and Jests from Delaware, Ohio." *HF* 7 (1948): 65–75.

———. "Folktales Collected in the Army." *CFQ* 3 (1944):115–120.

———. "John Darling, a New York Munchausen." *JAF* 57 (1944):97–106.

———. "Mountain Cowboy Folktales." *CFQ* 4 (1945):245–254.

———. "Tall Tales and Other Yarns from Calgary, Alberta." *CFQ* 4 (1945):29–49.

———, and Holaday, C. A. "Tall Tales and 'Sells' from Indiana University Students." *HFB* 2, no. 4 (December, 1944):59–65.

———, and Robinson, Emma. " 'Oregon' Smith: An Indiana Folk Hero." *SFQ* 6 (1942):163–168.

———, *et al.* "Folktales from Indiana University Students." *HFB* 1, no. 3 (December, 1942):85–97.

Hayeslip, Eleanor. "Sorting Our Tall Tales." *NYFQ* 1 (1945): 83–87.

Hoffman, Dan G. "Folk Tales of Paul Bunyan: Themes, Structure, Style, Sources." *WF* 9 (1950):312–320.

Key, Howard C. "Twister Tales." TXFS 28 (1958):52–68.

Larson, Mildred R. "The Taller the Better." *NYFQ* 18 (1962): 217–234.

Loomis, C. Grant. "The American Tall Tale and the Miraculous." *CFQ* 4 (1945):109–128. *An analysis of the Christian miracle tale and its relationship to other tales of the miraculous.*

† ———. "Jonathanisms: American Epigrammatic Hyperbole." *WF* 6 (1947):211–227.

———. "A Tall Tale Miscellany, 1830–1860." *WF* 6 (1947):28–41.

† Lunt, C. Richard K. "Jones Tracy: Tall Tale Teller from Mount Desert Island," chapter 3. *NEFL* 10 (1968):22–46. *Tales from the downeast region of Maine.*

† Masterson, James R. "Travelers' Tales of Colonial Natural History." *JAF* 59 (1946):174–188, 510–567.

O'Reilly, Edward. "Saga of Pecos Bill." *Century Magazine* (October, 1923):827–833.

Parks, H. B. "Razorbacks." TXFS 9 (1931):15–26.

† Parsons, Elsie Crews. "Spirituals and Other Folklore from the Bahamas." *JAF* 41 (1928):457–524.

† ———. "Tales from Guilford County, North Carolina." *JAF* 30 (1917):171–200.

Smith, Grace Partridge. "Egyptian 'Lies.'" *MF* 1 (1951):93–97. *Southern Illinois tales.*

———. "Folklore from Egypt." *JAF* 54 (1941):48–59. *Southern Illinois tales.*

———. "Tall Tales from Southern Illinois." *SFQ* 7 (1943):145–147.

Wilson, Robert. "Frozen Death." *The Old Farmer's Almanac* (1943): 50, 83.

Wyatt, P. J. "So-Called Tall Tales About Kansas." *WF* 22 (1963): 107–111.

Yates, Norris. "Some 'Whoppers' from the Armed Forces." *JAF* 62 (1949):173–180.

Zunser, Helen. "A New Mexican Village." *JAF* 48 (1935):125–178.

AN ACKNOWLEDGMENT

The following persons and organizations helped me to create this book:

Professor Kenneth S. Goldstein of the University of Pennsylvania, who made available his personal library of folklore.

Joseph C. Hickerson and his associates in the Folksong Section of the Library of Congress, who provided generous guidance and assistance in my research in the WPA archives.

Professor Esther K. Birdsall and Mrs. Geraldine Johnson of the University of Maryland, who made available resources of the Maryland Folklore Archives.

Professor Paolo Cucchi of Princeton University and Walter M. Gilbert, who made available important materials.

Librarians at the Bangor, Me., Public Library; the Denver Public Library; the Princeton, N.J., Public Library; and the libraries of the University of Maine, Princeton University, and Rutgers University.

Folklorists and folklore students whose research was a significant source of information and insight.

Students at Rutgers University who over the years have contributed to my folklore collection.

The children at Belmont School, Philadelphia, who shared their tales with me.

My daughters, Elizabeth and Nancy Schwartz, who helped decide what to include in this book and what to leave out.

My wife, Barbara Carmer Schwartz, who participated in the research.

Publishing firms which provided permission to use copyrighted materials.

To each I am deeply grateful.

A.S.

INDEX

Alvin Schwartz, drawing from his broad knowledge of folklore and folk life, has written more than twenty books for young readers. Among his many books are TELLING FORTUNES: *Love Magic, Dream Signs, and Other Ways to Learn the Future*; UNRIDDLING: *All Sorts of Riddles to Puzzle Your Guessery*, an ALA Notable Book; and A TWISTER OF TWISTS, A TANGLER OF TONGUES. Three of his most popular books are SCARY STORIES TO TELL IN THE DARK, MORE SCARY STORIES TO TELL IN THE DARK, and SCARY STORIES 3. He and his wife live in Princeton, New Jersey.

Glen Rounds spent his childhood on ranches in South Dakota and Montana. He attended art school in Kansas City, Missouri, and in New York City, and now lives in Southern Pines, North Carolina. He has illustrated many books for children, and has collaborated on five books with Alvin Schwartz, including A TWISTER OF TWISTS, A TANGLER OF TONGUES.

ALSO BY ALVIN SCHWARTZ AND GLEN ROUNDS

A Twister of Twists, A Tangler of Tongues

Tomfoolery: *Trickery and Foolery with Words*

Witcracks: *Jokes and Jests from American Folklore*

Cross Your Fingers, Spit in Your Hat:
Superstitions and Other Beliefs